PLANTING SEEDS

Story·Patricia Quinlan
Art·Vladyana Krykorka

Annick Press Ltd.
Toronto, Canada M2M 1H9

Annick Press gratefully acknowledges
the contributions of The Canada Council
and The Ontario Arts Council

Canadian Cataloguing in Publication Data

Quinlan, Patricia
    Planting seeds

ISBN 1-55037-007-3 (bound) ISBN 1-55037-006-5 (pbk.)

1. Conflict management – Juvenile literature.
2. Nuclear warfare – Psychological aspects –
Juvenile literature. I. Krykorka, Vladyana.
II. Title.

U263.Q56 1988   j303.6   C88-093194-9

Trade distribution in North America by:
Firefly Books Ltd.
3520 Pharmacy Avenue, Unit 1-C
Scarborough, Ontario
M1W 2T8

Printed and bound in Canada

To Dennis, with love

I was watching a T.V. show
about bombs.
I asked my mom,
"Why do people build bombs?"
She said, "To stop other people
from taking things away
from them."

I guess it's like when my brother
Matthew wants to share my toys
and I don't let him.

My mom says when Matthew and I are mad,
it's better to talk about it and not
hit each other. Sometimes,
that's hard. My mom says that
countries have to learn to talk
to each other too.

Sometimes I worry that the
whole world will blow up.
I feel scared when I think
about that. I don't know why
they had to invent the bomb.
I wish I could go back in time
and uninvent it.

I wanted to build a time machine.
I used our computer and an old
T.V. set. I wanted to program the
computer to use the pictures in
the T.V. set to send me back in time.
I tried and tried but it didn't work.
"It was a good idea, Rachel,"
my dad said.
I said, "I guess after something
has been done, we can't go back
and change it."

One night, I dreamed that someone dropped a bomb and everything was burning.
I screamed and my mom woke me. "I don't want everything to die, mommy," I said. I cried and my mom hugged me. "You're very precious to me, Rachel," she said.

One day, I found a
puppy that was lost.
He was very sick when
I found him. He hadn't
eaten for a long time.
Matthew and I took good
care of him and he got
better. My mom put an ad
in the paper and a lady came
to claim him. She was very
happy to see her puppy again.

When I first found the puppy,
he tried to bite me when I patted him.
He looked like he was afraid I was
going to hurt him. My mom said,
"Sometimes people are like that
too, Rachel. They hurt each
other because they're afraid."

I saw pictures in the newspaper
of kids who don't have enough to
eat. I felt sad for them.
"I wish someone would take care
of them," I said.
My dad looked sad too.
"If we all wanted to take care of each
other, we'd grow more food instead of
building bombs," he said.

I'm growing green beans in our garden for my science project. I planted lots of seeds. When they grow, I want to sell them and send the money to buy food for kids who don't have enough to eat. My dad says that planting seeds is very important.

Last night I had a dream.
I saw lots of hands holding the earth.
Some hands looked strong and kind,
like my dad's hands.
Some hands looked full of love,
like my mom's hands. Some hands
looked little, like my hands and
Matthew's hands. Then a voice said,
"We won't let everything die."

I still don't understand
about bombs very well,
but I understand about
planting seeds, and taking care
of each other, and talking to
Matthew when I'm mad. When I
feel scared about the bomb,
I'll think of my dream about
the hands holding the earth.

For Further Reading

The following titles were chosen primarily for their usefulness as vehicles
for discussion about conflict resolution.
The author wishes to thank the Canadian Children's Book Centre for their
assistance in compiling this list.

Ages 4 to 8:

Clancy's Coat
Eve Bunting
Illustrated by Lorinda Bryan Cauley. Frederick Warne, New York, 1984.
Tippitt and Clancy, two old friends who have quarrelled, gradually mend their friendship.

Good Times, Bad Times, Mummy and Me
Priscilla Galloway
Illustrated by Lissa Calvert. The Women's Press, Toronto, 1980.
A young girl struggles with feelings of love and hate toward her single, working mother.

I'll Make You Small
Tim Wynne-Jones
Illustrated by Maryann Kovalski, Groundwood Books, Toronto, 1986.
Roland wins the trust of Mr. Swanskin, a grouchy, reclusive neighbour.

Maggie and the Pirate
Ezra Jack Keats
Four Winds Press, New York, 1979.
Maggie comes to understand why the Pirate, a new kid, steals Niki, her pet cricket.

Mike and the Bike
Illustrated by Leoung O'Young
James Lorimer & Company, Toronto, 1980.
Jenny does not want Mike to touch her bike. But when some big kids try to steal it,
Jenny and Mike learn about both sharing and friendship.

My Dad Takes Care of Me
Patricia Quinlan
Illustrated by Vlasta Van Kampen. Annick Press, Toronto, 1987.
Luke is embarrassed to tell his friends that his dad is unemployed and there is
conflict when he wants a new bike that his family can't afford. These feelings are
worked through as Luke and his dad discover a new closeness and mutual
understanding.

The Pillow
Rosemary Allison

Illustrated by Charles Hilder. James Lorimer & Company, Toronto, 1979.
Angelina is very upset when some kids at school steal the pillow that Grandma Rosa
gave her before she left Italy to come to Canada. With Ram's help, Angelina gets her
pillow back and begins to make friends.

The Sandwich
Ian Wallace and Angela Wood

Kids Can Press, Toronto, 1975.
Vincenzo withdraws when his friends tease him about eating "stinky meat" but he
learns to stand up for himself and even persuades the others to try something new.
A useful book for a discussion about differences.

Sloan & Philamina or How To Make Friends with Your Lunch
Patti Stren

E.P. Dutton, New York, 1979.
Traditional enemies, an anteater and an ant, make friends and even help their
relatives to understand each other better.

The Streets are Free
Kurusa

Illustrated by Monica Doppert. Translation Karen Englander. Annick Press,
Toronto, 1985. (originally published by Ekare/Banco del Libro, Caracas, 1981)
The children of a Caracas barrio organize to get a playground. A useful book for a
discussion about how people can influence governments.

Waldo's Back Yard
Shirley Day

Annick Press, Toronto, 1984.
Waldo and Mr. Tester, an elderly neighbour, gain new understanding of each other
after their conflict about Waldo's back yard almost results in tragedy.

For Parents:

Facing The Nuclear Age, Parents and Children Together
Compiled by Susan Goldberg, PhD. Graphics by Molly Barker. Annick Press,
Toronto, 1985.
Susan Goldberg discusses how parents can help children cope with the fears and
anxieties of living in the nuclear age. Includes an excellent resource list of books
and films for younger and older children.